For all the Battersea Brownies –
past, present and future!

STRIPES PUBLISHING
An imprint of Magi Publications
1 The Coda Centre, 189 Munster Road,
London SW6 6AW

A paperback original. First published in Great Britain in 2010
Published by arrangement with Girlguiding UK
Brownie logo, uniforms and badges copyright © Girlguiding UK
Text copyright © Caroline Plaisted, 2010. Illustrations copyright © Katie Wood, 2010

ISBN: 978-1-84715-130-8

Find out more about the author at
www.carolineplaisted.com

Brownies

Circus Camp

Stripes

Meet the Brownies

Katie

Katie, Grace's twin, is super sporty and likes to play games and win. She wants to get every Brownie badge and her Six is Foxes!

Jamila

Jamila's got too many brothers, so she loves Brownies because NO BOYS ARE ALLOWED! Jamila is a Badger!

Ellie

Awesome at art and crafts, Ellie used to be a Rainbow and likes making new friends. Ellie is a Hedgehog!

Charlie

Animal-crazy Charlie has a guinea pig called Nibbles. She loves Brownie quizzes and Pow Wows. Her Six is Squirrels!

Grace

Grace is Katie's twin sister and she's ballet bonkers. Grace enjoys going on Brownie outings, and she is a Rabbit!

Chapter 1

We're Brownie Guides,
We're Brownie Guides,
We're here to lend a hand,
To love our God and serve our Queen
and help our homes and land.
We've Brownie friends,
We've Brownie friends in north, south,
east and west,
We're joined together in our wish
to try and do our best!

The 1st Badenbridge Brownies grinned as they settled down after their song. They couldn't wait to start the meeting.

"Hello, Brownies," said Vicky, one of the Brownie Leaders. "It's lovely to see you all."

"We've got an action-packed evening planned, based on the ideas you mentioned last week," added Sam, the other Leader.

"But first, we wanted to thank you for all your help at our open evening," Vicky continued.

"It was really good fun!" exclaimed Chloe, who was in Badgers with Jamila.

"Lots of people came, didn't they?" said Emma, the Sixer of the Foxes.

Like Brownies across the UK, the girls had been working towards a special badge called Adventure 100. It was to celebrate the Girlguiding UK Centenary and the Brownies

had the chance to take part in at least ten different challenges of their choice. They had recently completed Dance Dash – a special dance routine that had taken them all around town – to show everyone how brilliant Brownies was. They had also decided to hold an open evening where girls could come along and find out more about Brownies. So at their meeting the week before, the 1st Badenbridge Brownies had had lots of visitors. They had shown off their project and badge work as well as playing some great games and singing some songs with their guests.

"Did any of the girls that came say they wanted to join Brownies?" wondered Grace.

She'd felt especially important at the open

evening because she had been awarded her Dancer badge in front of everyone. She was now wearing it proudly on her sash.

"Quite a lot of them did," said Sam. "In fact, five girls are going to join us after half term."

There was a gasp of excitement from around the Ring, and Sam and Vicky laughed.

"It'll be great to have lots of new members, won't it?" said Vicky.

The Brownies nodded enthusiastically.

"Right! We need to talk about our unit camping trip," said Sam.

The hall buzzed with excited chatter.

"Daisy will be coming with us," explained Sam.

"And so will Ashvini's mum, Aruna, and my sister, Alex," said Vicky.

The Brownies cheered and Ashvini grinned, pleased that her mum would be coming camping too.

"Isn't Alex a Guide Leader?" asked Lauren, whose older sister was a Guide.

"She is." Vicky grinned.

"Wow!" said Charlie. "Is she going to be really strict?"

The Leaders giggled.

"Don't worry," said Vicky. "She might be my older sister but I promise she's lots of fun!"

"We've got a letter for you to take home with you," Sam explained. "It contains all the information your parents need about camp and asks them to come along to a meeting during next week's Brownie night. We'll give it to you at home time."

"Where will we be camping?" asked Pip, the newest 1st Badenbridge Brownie.

"A fantastic place called Waddow Hall in Lancashire," said Vicky. "It belongs to Girlguiding UK."

"You'll love it," said Daisy, who had visited Waddow Hall before. "There are lots of brilliant things to do there."

"What sort of things?" wondered Amber.

"Things like treks, games and sports. Plus we'll learn new skills!" exclaimed Molly, who had been on several Brownie camps.

"Yes," agreed Megan. "Last year we learned

to cook, we went swimming, and we wrote camp diaries too. If you haven't already got your Camper badge, maybe you can work on that while you're there."

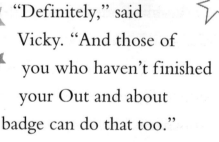

"Will I be able to do my Camper advanced badge, Vicky?" asked Molly.

"Definitely," said Vicky. "And those of you who haven't finished your Out and about badge can do that too."

"Yesss!" The happy Brownies grinned.

"Daisy is going to make a list of girls wanting to work on badges while we're at camp. She'll come round to your Six tables to ask what you'd like to do," said Sam.

"So why don't you take a look in your Badge Book to see what each badge involves? Oh – and don't forget that our camp will also count towards gaining the Adventure 100 badge at the end of the Centenary Year!"

"Now," said Vicky. "Talking about our camp leads us on to our first activity for tonight … a quiz!"

The Brownies loved quizzes!

"It's all about camping," said Sam. "Those of you who have been before will remember how important it is to follow camp rules."

"What camp rules?" asked Ellie, frowning.

"Things like keeping your tent and the campsite tidy so that it's safe. And helping out with the cooking and joining in the fun!" said Daisy. "Don't worry, you'll learn them in no time. And they're part of the Camper badge too."

"We want you to work together as a Six so that the older Brownies can help the younger ones answer the questions," said Vicky, handing out copies of the quiz.

"And when you've finished," added Sam, "you can all come back into the Ring so that we can talk through your answers. Ready?"

"Yesss!" yelled the excited Brownies, as they rushed off to their Sixes to begin.

Ellie was relieved to discover that the camp rules weren't at all hard to learn. When they had finished the quiz, the Brownies played one of their favourite games – Traffic Lights. Then, just before the meeting ended, Vicky asked some of the older girls to come and have a special Pow Wow with her.

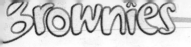

"What do you think they're up to?" Katie asked Lottie.

"Emma told me they're having a meeting to decide on the theme of our camp," she explained. "The older Brownies choose a theme every year. Last year it was animals... I wonder what it'll be this time?"

"Me too..." Katie replied thoughtfully.

Chapter 2

"So tell us!" Katie urged. "What's the theme for our camp, Boo?"

It was Thursday afternoon, and the five best friends were sitting in Charlie's room, chatting about their next big Brownie adventure. Boo, Charlie's older sister, was with them.

"I can't tell you!" Boo replied. "I'm sworn to secrecy."

"Oh, go on!" said Charlie. "It's *so* not fair that you know already!"

The other girls agreed. But Boo's lips were sealed.

"If I told you, then I'd be breaking my

promise to Vicky and Sam," she explained.
"Anyway, you'll find out soon."

Jamila sighed. "Oh, I can't wait! Camp's
going to be such fun!"

"Won't it be cold, though?" wondered
Ellie. "You know, sleeping outside?"

"Well, our tent was warm and cosy when
Katie and I went camping with Mum and
Dad," Grace pointed out. "Haven't you been
camping before, Ellie?"

"Never," said Ellie. "And I'm not really
sure I like the idea of it. It's going to be so
dark at night! Plus there will be all those
spiders and creepy-crawlies – yuck!"

"I was worried before I went on my first
Brownie camp," said Boo. "I thought I was
going to find a snake in my sleeping bag!"

"Oh, please tell me there aren't any *snakes*
at Waddow Hall!" shrieked Ellie.

All the girls giggled.

"Course not!" said Boo. "Brownie campsites are really comfortable, with real loos and toasty-warm tents. We'll have fun and play games and discover loads of new things. I love Brownie camp – and you will too!"

"Do you think so?" Ellie asked, not quite convinced.

"Definitely!" said Boo. "Hey – I'll go and fetch my camp diary from last year so you can see what we got up to."

"Don't worry, Ellie," Jamila said soothingly, as Boo whizzed off to her bedroom. "This will be the first Brownie camp for all five of us. None of us know what it's going to be like."

"But we'll all be there together, and we know that Vicky and Sam are going to make sure it's mega fun!" Grace added.

"Yes," said Charlie. "Plus Alex the Guide Leader will be there too. How cool is that!"

Boo returned, carrying a notebook.

"Take a look," she said, handing it to Ellie. "You have to write in it every day you're at camp. At first, I thought it might be boring, but it's actually fun to write about what you get up to."

The girls flicked through the book, which was full of photographs and drawings of happy Brownies having all sorts of fun.

"Wow, you did archery!" cried Katie.

"And you look like you're playing a brilliant game here," Jamila pointed out.

"*Everything* is brilliant at Brownie camp," declared Boo. "You get to meet lots of Brownies from other units all over the country. I made so many new friends and laughed so much."

"I remember when you came home," said Charlie. "You went straight to bed and didn't get up until lunchtime the next day!"

Boo giggled. "Well, I was exhausted! Listen, Ellie – you are going to *love* camp. Especially with this year's theme." She winked teasingly. Just then, Boo heard her mum calling from downstairs. "Gotta go.

I promised I'd help with Georgia. Bye!"

"See you!" the others replied.

"Camp's going to be amazing," Grace said.
"Just think of all the new badges we can
work on while we're there!"

"It'll be great to finish the Out and about
badge," Charlie replied. "It was the first one
we started when we joined Brownies!"

"I've almost forgotten what we have to do
to finish it," said Grace.

"Let's check in here," Charlie
said, picking up her Badge
Book. "I was reading up on it
in bed last night."

The Brownies checked
through the list of tasks. They'd
already been on a scavenger hunt with their
unit, and done a poster about keeping safe
when out and about.

"I guess we'll learn what to wear for a walk and how to read a map at camp," said Ellie.

"How about the Camper badge?" asked Katie. "What does it say about that?"

Charlie thumbed through the pages.

"Here it is," she said. "OK. Obviously, we have to go camping … do a new activity while we're there … write a diary and make a keepsake…"

Grace looked over Charlie's shoulder. "And help with cooking and clearing away. And collect water and wood…" she said.

"…And know how to keep yourself, the tent and the things inside it dry," said Charlie.

"Brilliant!" said Katie. "I can't wait to get another badge. I've only got a couple more things to do on my Sports badge too!"

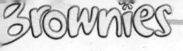

"And I've nearly finished my Friend to animals badge," said Charlie.

"How about your Artist badge, Ellie?" asked Grace. "You've worked so hard on it, you can't have that much more left to do."

"I haven't," Ellie agreed. "I just have one more painting to complete. Oh, and I'm entering it into the Badenbridge Art Competition too. It's being held this Saturday in the town hall. Mum and I only found out about it last week, and I've had to really rush to do my painting in time!"

"Wow!" exclaimed Katie. "What have you painted?"

24

"Well, it had to be something in Badenbridge, so since we'd climbed the town hall clock tower, I decided to paint a picture of the town hall," Ellie replied. "But I haven't quite finished it yet. That's why Mum's coming to pick me up early – I've got to get home and do the final bits. She has to take it to the town hall tomorrow morning!"

"So is your painting going to be on display at the weekend?" asked Grace.

"Yes!" Ellie blushed. "I hope it looks good."

"Your paintings are always brilliant, Ellie," encouraged Jamila.

"We'll ask Dad if we can come along to the exhibition and see it, won't we, Grace?" said Katie.

"You bet!" her sister confirmed.

"Boo and I won't be able to come!" Charlie groaned. "We're going to visit Gran this weekend."

"Sorry, Ellie, I won't be able to make it either," said Jamila. "I've got my piano exam on Saturday – I'm *so* nervous about it! But if I pass I'll have completed my Musician badge."

Grace smiled. "That's fantastic news, Jamila!"

Just then, the doorbell went.

"That'll be my mum now," said Ellie, jumping up.

"Good luck with your painting! It'll definitely be the best one." Grace grinned.

"Thanks. And I know you'll be brilliant in your exam, Jamila," said Ellie.

"Yes! Good luck to both of you!" Katie cheered, as Ellie waved and disappeared downstairs.

The weekend was so busy it passed in a flash! On Monday morning, Ellie, Charlie, Jamila, Katie and Grace had a lot of catching up to do before school started.

"Hey – there's Jamila!" Grace said excitedly to her sister as they waited in the playground.

Just then, Ellie arrived. "Hello!" she said, dashing over to her friends.

"Wait for me!" called Charlie, running into the playground behind her. "So tell us! How was the exam, Jamila?"

"OK, I think. The examiner was really friendly." Jamila smiled. "I'll get the result later this week. But Ellie – what happened at the art exhibition?"

"You can't believe how amazing her picture was!" Grace said.

"Yes," added Katie. "It was absolutely brilliant – which is probably why Ellie won Best in Show for the children's competitions!"

"Wow!" shrieked the others. "Well done, Ellie!"

Ellie blushed. "Thanks! It was so cool – I got a trophy *and* a certificate!"

Ding-aling-aling-aling-aling!

"Oh no – the bell," sighed Grace.

"And I wanted to hear more about Jamila's exam – and the art competition too," Charlie added.

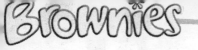

"Good job you're all coming round to our house for tea after school," said Katie. "We can catch up on everything then."

"And it's a good job I've been making scrummy flapjacks with my gran this weekend," Charlie pointed out. "I'll bring them along with me for us to nibble on!"

Chapter 3

After school, the best friends headed to the twins' house. They were so excited about camp they couldn't stop talking about it. As the five girls munched on Charlie's delicious flapjacks, they chatted about what they were going to pack in their rucksacks and wondered what the camp theme was going to be. And before everyone went home, Charlie promised to get the flapjack recipe from her gran so the girls could bake them together sometime.

On Tuesday night, the five girls joined the rest of their unit in the hall. Their parents and carers were also there, waiting for the special meeting with Vicky and Sam.

After a few minutes of excited chatter, the
Brownie Leaders stood in the middle of the
hall and put up their right hands. Aruna,
Ashvini's mum, was with them, because she
was helping at their meeting that night. The
Brownies fell silent and put up their right
hands as well.

"Thank you, everyone," said Sam. "Let's all get ourselves into the Brownie Ring and begin."

Quickly, the Brownies seated themselves on the floor. As always, their Pow Wow began with some of the girls telling their special news. Izzy, the Sixer of the Badgers, told them about a book she'd just read. She thought the rest of the Brownies would enjoy it too because it was about a Brownie. Poppy and Jamila mentioned that they'd both done music exams, and Ellie, of course, told them about her success in the art competition.

"Well done, Ellie! We'll award you your Artist badge at the next meeting. But in the meantime, I think you deserve a clap!" declared Vicky.

The Brownies gave her a round of applause.

Sam smiled. "You are always such busy girls. It's great to hear everything you've been up to. Now … who's looking forward to camp?"

"Meee!" cheered every Brownie in the room.

"Good!" Sam giggled. "As you know, Vicky and I will be having a meeting with the grown-ups in a minute to talk about our trip. But first, we have a bit of news for you."

"When we go on our annual camp," Vicky continued, "Sam and I like to give it a theme. Each year, we ask our older Brownies to help us choose it, based on the things you all enjoy."

The best friends looked at each other in excitement. Time to reveal Boo's secret!

"Our theme this year is … the circus!" Vicky announced.

"Oh, I love the circus!" said Caitlin.

"So we are going to learn some circus skills while we are at Waddow Hall," said Sam. "And, if you would like to, some of you could work towards earning your Circus performer badge, alongside your Camper badge. Does that sound good?"

"Yesss!" the girls agreed.

"Are we going to start learning circus skills now?" Grace wanted to know.

"Not today," Vicky replied. "But you are going to make something that you will need to learn to juggle – a beanbag!"

Katie was especially pleased to hear this, because she had already taught herself to juggle for the Brownie show that they'd done at their unit sleepover. Now she'd be able to help the others learn how to juggle too!

The Brownies started to chatter excitedly. They wanted to get crafting!

Vicky and Sam put up their hands and the girls fell silent again.

"Now, our meeting with the grown-ups will start in a minute," Vicky said, as she looked at her watch. "Aruna and Daisy are going to show you how to make your beanbags and—"

But before she could finish, another adult wearing Leaders' clothes walked into the hall.

"Ooops!" she said, putting her hand to her mouth. "Sorry to interrupt your Pow Wow, Brownies!"

The lady came over to the Brownie Ring.

"This is Alex," said Sam, smiling. "She's also going to speak with the adults tonight."

"Hello!" said the Brownies.

"Hello!" Alex grinned. "I'm really looking forward to getting to know you all when we go camping!"

The Brownies smiled at her. She seemed friendly and fun.

"Right then," said Vicky. "We'd better be off. Have fun making those beanbags, girls!"

Aruna and Daisy explained that making the beanbags was easy. First, they took a piece of rectangular felt and stuck felt shapes on it to make a clown's face. Then they sewed that piece to another rectangle of felt, leaving just the one side open. After filling the bag with hard, dry beans, they sewed it up and – *ta-daa* – they had a beanbag!

The Brownies went to their Six tables and were soon busy working away. Around the hall, the girls chatted about camp as they worked. They all wanted to make two beanbags to juggle with, but not everyone managed to finish their second one before

Vicky, Sam and Alex came back.

"How are you getting on?" asked Alex, as the Leaders came to look at their handiwork. "Wow! These look great. I hope you will all join my Guide unit one day – we need your talent!"

The Brownies grinned happily.

"Now, girls," said Vicky, clapping her hands. "I'm afraid we are running out of time."

"But I haven't finished yet!" Charlie replied.

"Nor me!" said lots of the others.

"Well," Sam said, "we can either carry on with the beanbags or play a game before home time – your choice."

"A game!" the Brownies cheered.

"OK then," said Vicky. "Take the beanbags with you to finish off at home – just don't forget to bring them to camp!"

The Brownies quickly cleared away, ready to play.

"This is a circus game to get us in the mood for camp," said Vicky. "It's called Clowning About."

"How do we play?" asked Grace.

"Imagine the hall is a Big Top. When I shout 'Clowns', you have to run over to the front," explained Sam. "If I say 'Trapeze', rush over to the corner. 'Unicycles' are by the cupboard, and 'Ring Master' is over at the windows."

"The last girl to reach each area, and anyone who goes to the wrong place, is out," said Vicky. "Last person in the Big Top is the winner!"

The hall buzzed with enthusiasm.

"Ready?" asked Vicky. "Clowns!"

Two days later, on Thursday evening, Ellie, Jamila, Charlie, Katie and Grace gathered together to finish off their beanbags at Jamila's house. As they worked, they talked

41

about what they'd packed in their rucksacks, ready to leave for camp the next day.

"I don't understand why we have to take a whole set of clothes that we won't even use in a separate bag!" said Katie.

"It is a *bit* weird," Jamila said.

"Mum says that you have to give them to Vicky and Sam when we get to camp," explained Charlie. "It's an emergency set of clothes in case something happens to your other ones. But no one ever needs to use them."

"What could possibly happen to *all* your other clothes?" Grace wondered.

"Oh, I don't even want to think about it," sighed Ellie, looking a bit glum. "I've never spent a whole weekend away from my mum before. I'm really going to miss her."

"Course you will," said Jamila, putting her arm around her friend. "But you are also going to have a really great time with us! Remember how much you enjoyed the Brownie sleepover?"

"Yes!" Charlie agreed. "We won't have time to think about home."

"You'll be too busy having juggling lessons with me!" announced Katie, who had finished her second beanbag and was showing off her skills.

"Oooops…"

Her beanbags tumbled to the floor. The others laughed.

"Looks like you need a bit more practice!" Ellie said.

Katie giggled and shrugged her shoulders, then sat down with the other girls.

"Hey, I was talking to Chloe at school," Jamila said. "She's going to bring her guitar to camp so that she can play while we sing songs around the campfire."

"Cool!" said Grace. "Do you think you'll hear about your piano exam soon, Jamila?"

"Oh, I nearly forgot!" Jamila exclaimed. "Mum told me when I got home from school this afternoon – I passed!"

Katie grinned. "That's brilliant news!"

"Well done!" Jamila's other friends agreed.

"Isn't it great?" said Charlie. "Not only is it half term next week, but we're going on Brownie camp tomorrow. And now Jamila's passed her piano exam as well!"

"Yesss!" the girls cheered.

Chapter 4

As soon as the Badenbridge Primary School
bell went on Friday afternoon, all the girls
who were Brownies rushed home. And they
had a good reason to hurry – they were off
to fetch their kit for camp!

By five o'clock, all the
Brownies were gathered
outside the school,
dressed in their Brownie
clothes, ready for camp.

Everyone was busy:
the girls helped the
adults to load their
bags into the luggage

store of the bus, while Vicky ticked everyone's names off her list, and Sam and Alex made sure all the girls had their things with them.

"Thanks for bringing us, Mum!" said Katie, giving her a hug. "We'll see you on Sunday – bye!"

Katie hopped on to the bus. She was desperate to bag the back seat. That was the only way the five best friends could sit together for the journey!

"Have a great time," said her mum, as she hugged Grace. "Be good and keep your tent tidy."

"We will!" Grace giggled ... but then her face fell as she spotted Ellie, who was hugging her mum, tears pouring down her face.

"It's only for a couple of nights," her mum said. "You'll have Cuddlebear to snuggle up to and you'll have a great time."

"I don't think I want to go!" sighed Ellie, wiping her eyes. "I mean, I want to go – but I want you to come with us!"

"Oh, sweetie," soothed her mum. "I can't – there isn't enough room on the bus for me as well."

Grace and Jamila rushed over.

"Come on, Ellie," said Grace. "We're going to have such a great time – if you don't come with us, it won't be fun at all!"

"We need you," Jamila agreed. "How are we going to be able to do all the craft stuff without you?"

Ellie wiped her nose with a hanky.

Just then, Charlie and Boo arrived. Their bags were already on the bus and they were about to climb aboard too.

"Ready for our camping adventure?" Charlie asked. "Look – Katie's saved the best seats! We'd better be quick or someone else might grab them. Coming, Ellie?"

Ellie looked at her friends and then her mum. She was really going to miss her … but then she didn't want to miss her friends and all the adventures either.

"Yes!" she declared, giving her mum one final hug.

"Come on then," said Grace. "Let's go!"

A short while later, everyone was sitting on the bus, ready to set off.

"I'm just going to do a quick head count," announced Vicky. With her clipboard in her

hand, she walked up the aisle of the bus, counting Brownies.

"OK." She grinned. "All here! Now, have you buckled your seat belts? Are the adults ready?"

"Yes!" everyone cheered.

"Well, let's go then!"

And the 1st Badenbridge Brownies bus left for camp!

The Brownies were in holiday mood, singing songs and playing games of 'I-Spy' as the bus headed out of town. When they'd run out of things to 'spy', Sam suggested they watch a film she'd brought with her. Soon, the bus fell silent as the Brownies watched the movie, entranced.

The rest of the journey passed in a flash.

Then Molly shouted out, "Hey, look! We're here – there's Waddow Hall!"

The bus buzzed with excitement as the Brownies looked out at where they would be camping for the weekend – a huge old manor house overlooking a river and surrounded by beautiful countryside as far as the eye could see.

After grabbing their bags, the Brownies
followed the grown-ups to the field where
they would be camping. Other Brownie
and Guide units were set up in tents in the
surrounding fields.

"Our tents are already here!" said Katie.

"Oh good," Grace said. "I was worried
that we'd have to put them up ourselves!"

"I wonder which one we'll sleep in?"
said Ellie.

But before any of her friends could answer,
they spotted that the Leaders had their right
hands up. The Brownies put down their bags
and did the same, falling silent.

"Thanks, girls," said Vicky. "Welcome to
this year's First Badenbridge Brownie camp!"

"Isn't it exciting to be here at last! Now,

Brownies

we need to tell you where you'll be sleeping," Sam said, checking her clipboard.

"Can we have this tent, please?" asked Katie, pointing to a tent next to a large oak tree.

"I'm afraid that's the Leaders' tent," said Sam. "Daisy is going to put the Six signs up on the other tents for us. When she's done that, find your Six tent and sort out your sleeping bags, please."

"But I thought we would all be together!" Charlie exclaimed, looking round at her friends.

"So did I!" wailed Ellie.

"Never mind," said Jamila, giving her a hug. "We'll be so tired when we go to bed, we won't have time to miss each other. Come on – let's sort our stuff out."

The girls disappeared into their tents. They

54

unpacked their night stuff and unrolled their
sleeping bags on to the camp beds that were
already set up inside. Daisy and the adults had
each been given one Six tent to be Camp
Leader for. Daisy was in charge of the Foxes,
Aruna the Squirrels, Vicky took care of the
Rabbits, Alex looked after the Hedgehogs,
and Sam checked on the Badgers.

Each Camp Leader explained to their
Six that it was important to keep their tent
tidy. It was also essential to make sure their
things never touched the sides, because if it
rained, anything touching the walls of the
tent might get wet. Plus, there was going to
be a competition for the tidiest tent and the
Leaders were going to carry out inspections
without warning!

Inside the Hedgehog tent, Ellie was
searching frantically through her bag.

"What's up?" asked Poppy. "Lost something?"

"Yes!" she wailed. "Cuddlebear! I must have left him in Mum's car."

"Hey, don't worry," said Lauren, her Sixer. "Here – why don't you have Prickles for when you go to sleep?" Prickles was the Hedgehogs' fluffy toy mascot. "I know it's not the same, but he can still snuggle up with you."

"Thanks," said Ellie, feeling better. Being with other Brownies meant that any problem was soon solved.

After organizing their tents, the Brownies were asked to give their emergency clothing bags to the Leaders. Then they all gathered together outside.

"When are we going to start learning our Circus skills?" Chloe asked eagerly.

"Not tonight," replied Sam. "After that long journey, we're all probably feeling a bit tired, aren't we?"

"Yes," Pip said. "But I'm ever so excited about being here!"

The other Brownies agreed.

"We're going to have a special Pow Wow in a little while," said Vicky. "That'll give us a chance to tell you all about what will happen during camp."

"But first we have an important job to do," revealed Sam. "Which is to make up the campfire."

"Cool!" said the Brownies.

"So, each Six needs to go with their Camp Leader to gather firewood from under the trees around the field," Vicky explained. "Let's see how much we can gather in ten minutes! Ready? Steady? Go!"

Chapter 5

The Brownies were amazed at how quickly they collected enough firewood.

"The Leaders are experts at this camping stuff," said Grace, as they all stood back to watch Sam light the kindling. Flames soon began to lick and crackle at the twigs they'd all helped to gather.

"Right," said Alex, as the fire took hold. "Make sure you all keep a good distance away, won't you?"

The Brownies nodded.

"That's one of our camping rules," Vicky said. "This seems a good time for us to have our Pow Wow so we can remind you of all the others. We've got some sitters for everyone to get comfy on – Daisy will hand them out."

Quickly, the girls helped to spread the sitters out around the campfire before settling down in a Brownie Ring. They smiled when Aruna and the other Leaders all joined them on the ground instead of sitting on chairs like they did back in the hall.

The 1st Badenbridge Brownies began their

Pow Wow with a song. Afterwards, Sam explained that whilst they were at camp it was important that everyone, Brownies and Leaders, followed the camp rules.

"Obviously," she said, "there should be no running near the fire or getting too close to it. Even when it has burned down in the morning, the ground and the cinders could still be very hot!"

"We talked about other camp rules before we came," Vicky pointed out. "Who can remember what they are?"

A sea of hands quickly shot up.

"Teamwork," said Katie.

"Yes, always making sure we help out with everything," added Poppy.

"And keeping our tents and the camp area tidy," Ellie said.

"Ohhh!" said an impatient Izzy, waving her hand in the air. "Do our share of the cooking and washing up afterwards."

"Plus we've got to help gather wood – and get water too!" Charlie added.

"And we should never wander away from our camp area on our own," Boo pointed out. "If we need to go anywhere we must ask permission from one of the Leaders."

"Well done, Brownies." Sam grinned.

"I can see that you are well prepared – you're going to have a great camp."

The Brownies smiled.

"Now, hands up who's doing their Brownie camper badge this weekend?" asked Vicky.

Lots of Brownies, including Ellie, Katie, Jamila, Charlie and Grace, put their hands up.

"Those girls doing their Advanced camper badge, remember who has their hand up," said Vicky. "You already know that part of gaining your badge is helping the girls who haven't camped before. Explain how to do things so that we all stay safe and dry, and have lots of fun!"

The older Brownies, including Boo, sat up straight, feeling important.

"Now," said Sam. "You all know that you'll be keeping a diary while you are at camp. Aruna is going to hand them out now.

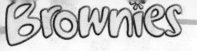

Make sure you put your name on the cover."

"You can write about anything you like – your favourite activities, things you've learned, or perhaps things that have made you laugh," Vicky explained, as Aruna handed out the notebooks. "Just don't forget to write in them every day!"

"We'll start learning our circus skills tomorrow," said Vicky. "But now it's time for dinner! Aruna has drawn up a rota and each Six will be responsible for taking a share in all the chores this weekend. Come and ask her what job you can help with now, and let's get supper going!"

With everyone's help, the meal was soon ready. There were sausages, veggie burgers and baked beans. The Brownies tucked in

hungrily as they sat around the campfire.

"That was yummy!" Jamila said, as she finished her last mouthful of beans.

"The best meal I've ever eaten," said Grace.

"I didn't realize that camp food would be this good," said Ellie, licking her lips.

"Come on," said Charlie. "We've got to help wash up!"

"Oh yes," agreed Katie. "Quick!"

Normally, the girls didn't think that doing chores like washing-up was much fun. But at camp, things were different! The Brownies and their Leaders worked as a team, sharing the jobs between them. The campsite was tidy again in no time at all.

"Oh!" said Charlie. "I've just had an idea! Back in a sec." She rushed off in the direction of the tents, while her friends settled down on the sitters around the fire.

Charlie reappeared a moment later. "Hey, everyone – say cheese!" She held up her camera and snapped a photo of her friends.

"Here," said Aruna. "Why don't I take a group photo of you?"

"Oh, yes, please!" said Charlie.

The five best friends huddled together. "Cheese!" they said, smiling as the camera flash went.

As the girls thanked Aruna, Alex sat down beside them. "Are you having fun?" she asked.

"Yes!" they replied.

"Hey, Alex, do you take Guides on camp?" Katie asked.

"I certainly do," said Alex. "Sometimes we go away for a whole week."

"What other things do Guides do?" wondered Charlie.

Alex told them all about projects the Guides had done, their special badges, outings and craftwork. "Most girls start at Guides when they are ten," she explained, "when they leave Brownies. Perhaps you will too."

The girls nodded in agreement. Just then, Chloe sat down with her guitar, and the Leaders suggested singing some camp songs. Everyone joined in, having a great time.

The Brownies sang all their favourite songs, but after a while, they began to yawn.

Sam smiled. "Time for bed, I think." And for once, none of the Brownies disagreed.

"OK, girls," said Vicky. "Let's put away our sitters and then head for the wash block."

The Brownies grabbed their washbags, and were soon brushing their teeth and queueing to use the loos. There were other Brownies already in the wash block when they arrived. Just like the 1st Badenbridge Brownies, they were giggling and having fun with their friends.

"Hey, I recognize those girls," Grace whispered to Katie.

One of the girls walked over to them, smiling. "Hello!" she said. "Aren't you camping at the other end of our field?"

"Yes," said Katie. "That one over there."

She pointed to their camp.

"Cool!" the girl said. "I'm Gemma, by the way. We're from the Fourth Agnestown Brownies. We arrived today for a canoeing and watersport weekend. How about you?"

The five friends quickly introduced themselves and their unit, and chatted with Gemma and her friends about their circus camp.

"That sounds great! Well, we'd better get back to our tents now," said Gemma. "See you around though. Night!"

"Night!" the girls replied.

When they had brushed their teeth, the Brownies made their way back to camp, following Daisy and Aruna.

"I know we've only just got here," said Charlie, "but I'm already loving it!"

"It's great, isn't it?" agreed Katie.

"Are you having fun, Ellie?" Jamila asked.

"Well… I wish I had Cuddlebear with me," Ellie sighed, her bottom lip trembling.

"I know. But at least you've got Prickles to snuggle up with," said Grace, as they arrived back at their tents.

Ellie nodded.

"Come on, girls, into bed," Vicky called.

Tucked up in their cosy sleeping bags, most of the Brownies fell asleep quickly. But, in the Hedgehogs' tent, Ellie lay in the darkness, wide awake. She was thinking of her mum, and Cuddlebear.

"Are you still up, Ellie?" Lauren, her Sixer whispered.

"Yeah," Ellie sighed.

In the darkness, the pair chatted quietly about their day. Ellie was glad someone else was awake, but after talking for a little while, she began to yawn.

"Are you still awake?" whispered Lauren.

There was no answer – Ellie had fallen asleep. Pleased, Lauren closed her own eyes and nodded off too.

Chapter 6

The next morning, the Brownies woke to a bright and sunny day. All the girls helped to make delicious porridge and scrambled eggs for breakfast. As they cleaned up afterwards, the five best friends waved across the field to their new friend, Gemma.

"Right, girls! Grab the sitters," said Sam. "It's time for a Pow Wow."

Once everyone had settled down, Vicky explained that they were going on a tour of the Waddow Hall estate.

"But before we go," Sam said, hushing the excited girls, "Molly, Boo and Izzy are going to remind us of the Country Code.

We've talked about it at Brownies before, but we all need to think about it as we walk."

The three older girls stood up.

"We must be safe by planning ahead and following any signs," said Boo.

"Leave gates and property as you find them, and consider other people," added Molly.

"Protect plants and animals," warned Izzy. "And put your litter in the bin or take it home with you."

"Thank you, girls." Vicky grinned. "There is one other thing in the Country Code, which is to keep dogs under control, but I don't think we've brought any puppies with us!"

The Brownies laughed.

"We're going to split up into our Sixes to go and explore," said Sam. "Find your Six Leader and then we'll all meet up back here a bit later."

"I can't believe how much there is to do here!" Charlie said to her friends when they got back to camp. "Look at all the photos I took."

"The house is huge!" exclaimed Jamila.

"I know," said Ellie. "I bought some postcards in the shop to show my mum."

"So did I," Charlie said. "I'm going to send one to Gran."

"I had no idea there were four other campsites here as well," said Grace.

"Hey," said Katie. "What are Vicky and Sam up to?"

The girls turned to see the Leaders heading for the Six tents.

"It's a tent inspection," said Daisy, who was sitting with them. "They'll be doing that a lot this weekend!"

"I hope our tent is tidy enough," Ellie said.

The girls continued to chat about all the things they'd seen on their tour. They'd spotted the Agnestown girls canoeing, and other Brownies pond dipping and cycling.

"I wish I could stay here forever and do everything!" Katie sighed.

"There'll be lots of other camps to go on," said Daisy. "And as you get older, you'll get a chance to do things like canoeing, too."

Just then, Vicky and Sam came out of the last tent and put up their right hands. The Brownies waited expectantly.

"I know it was only your first tent inspection," said Vicky, "but some of them were a little bit messy."

"It's really important to keep your bedding and clothing off the floor, girls," Sam warned. "If you don't, they could get wet and muddy!"

"Anyway," Vicky continued, "the best tent this morning is … the Foxes! They get to keep our Brownie mascot, Beryl, until the next inspection."

"Yesss!" the Foxes cried, as Emma, their Sixer, collected their prize. Beryl was a rag doll dressed as a Brownie. She even had a miniature trefoil badge on her top!

"I wonder which Six will win her next?" Vicky said. "Now, it's time to get your Brownie day packs ready – and don't forget your diaries. We're off on a walk to collect treasures."

The Brownies had learned what to put in a day pack when they did their Out and about badges.

"What does she mean, 'treasures'?" Jamila wanted to know.

"Let's find out!" Grace replied, rushing off to her tent.

The Leaders split the Brownies into two groups. One was led by Sam, Aruna and Daisy, and the other girls went with Vicky and Alex. Before they set off, Vicky explained that they should collect interesting-looking twigs, leaves and other natural treasures as they explored the countryside.

"As part of your Camper badge, you need to make a souvenir of your trip," Daisy added. "So we thought you could make a collage or a model with things gathered from the grounds."

"Yes!" said Ellie. This project was exactly the sort of thing she loved to do.

So, after checking that everyone had remembered to pack their waterproof coats, their water bottles and their diaries, the two groups set off in different directions. Each group had a map, and the Brownies had to make sure they were following the right path.

It turned out that Jamila and Grace's group were good at finding beautiful leaves and interesting twigs but weren't that good at

map reading and, at one point, they took the wrong footpath and ended up in the wrong place completely.

"We're meant to be at a viewpoint now," pointed out Boo, who was in their group.

"Oh!" sighed Molly, her Sixer. "Let's have a look at the map again… I've got it! There was a fork in the path back there." She pointed to the map. "We should have followed the other bit of it. Come on! Let's retrace our steps."

So that's exactly what they did. They soon found themselves standing at the top of a hill, looking at a most spectacular view across the whole of the Waddow Hall estate.

"Wow! This is amazing," said Jamila, and everyone agreed. "I can see the Agnestown Brownies on the river – look!"

"Oh yes!" said the others.

"Hey, look!" urged Grace. "Isn't that the others over there!"

She pointed across to another group of
Brownies in the distance, who seemed to
have spotted them at exactly the same time.
The two sets of Brownies waved at each
other enthusiastically.

In the group on the opposite side of the
valley, Katie wondered, "Do you think
that means they've got halfway as well?
We'd better hurry up and get back to camp
before they do!"

"But it isn't a race," Charlie pointed out. "And I still need to find lots more leaves. I haven't got many."

"Come on, girls," said Vicky, who was leading their group. "Let's follow our map back to camp. We can still gather things as we go. It's muddy up ahead so mind where you step!"

They trod carefully, collecting things as they went.

Ellie picked up a delicate leaf. "I can't wait to get started on my model – ugh!"

She'd been so busy thinking about her model, Ellie hadn't looked where she was walking. Vicky had said it was muddy, but none of them had expected it to be quite so boggy.

"Gross!" said Poppy, trying to tiptoe across the mud.

Katie held Pip's hand as she stepped across a huge puddle. Charlie and Ellie were following them across a muddy stretch when Ellie decided if she went round the far side of one of the trees, it would be less slippery. That was a big mistake…

"Oh no!" she wailed.

"Come on!" urged Katie. "Follow us."

"I can't!" Ellie replied. "My foot's stuck!"

Vicky and Alex came over to help.

"Oh dear!" said Alex. "We'd better pull you out. Here, take my hand."

She gave a tug and Ellie was released from the mud – minus her shoe!

With one leg in the air, Ellie bent down to retrieve it.

"Ooops!" Ellie wobbled – and then fell over into the sloppy, muddy puddle. She burst into tears.

Alex and Vicky whisked Ellie up and out
of the mud, and Katie, Charlie and the other
girls rushed over to help.

"Oh, Ellie, are you OK?" asked Charlie.

Ellie wiped the tears and mud from her face.

"I want to go home!" she wailed.

Chapter 7

Jamila, Grace and all the other Brownies
were surprised when the second group
eventually returned to camp.

"Oh no!" Jamila exclaimed when she saw
the state Ellie was in.

"What happened?" asked Grace, rushing
over, and Katie explained.

"I'll come with you to the wash block,"
said Jamila, following Vicky as she led the
mud-soaked Ellie away.

"Can you take her emergency clothes with
you, please?" asked Sam, handing them over.

"So that's why we needed to bring
them," said Grace, as she watched Ellie go.

85

Charlie sighed. "Ellie says she wants to go home. We know she's missing her mum, and now she's got all wet and yucky, she said she's had enough of camping."

"Well, we have to do our best to make her stay," Katie declared. "Camp won't be the same without her!"

The Brownies busied themselves by making sandwiches for lunch whilst they waited for Ellie and Jamila to return.

"Hey, look what's over there!" said Caitlin, pointing to the Leaders' tent.

"Yoyos and diabolos!" said Bethany.

"And some flowerpot stilts as well," Pip added. "I used ones like that at a party once."

"That must be our circus skills stuff!" said Katie.

Word spread amongst the Brownies – they couldn't wait to start learning how to use them.

So it was fortunate that a much drier, cleaner Ellie reappeared in camp with Jamila soon afterwards.

"Are you OK?" asked Charlie.

"Yeah, thanks." Ellie smiled weakly.

"It's a good thing you're back – we need you to help us learn how to use the flowerpot stilts," said Katie.

"I'm not sure I want to stay, though," sighed Ellie. "I just want to call Mum to come and get me."

"But we need you!" said Charlie.

"Yes! You've got to stay!" Katie, Grace and Jamila all spoke at once. Then all five girls began to giggle.

"Please say you'll stay?" begged Jamila.

Ellie looked at her best friends, then slowly smiled. "OK then. As long as I don't get wet again!"

Just then, the Brownie Leaders raised their right hands and everyone stopped what they were doing.

"Before we have our picnic, we've got some time to learn how to be circus performers!" said Sam.

"Yesss!" the Brownies cheered.

Vicky explained. "Alex, Sam, Daisy, Aruna and I are going to look after one activity each. If you fancy learning how to juggle, fetch the beanbags you made from your tents, and then see Aruna. Diabolo and devil-stick skills will be taught by Alex. If stilts are your thing, then see Sam. Daisy is our expert on the hoopla. But if you want to learn to do magic with scarves, that's with me!"

"But I want to do everything!" Katie exclaimed, making everyone laugh.

"Well, we'd better get started then!" Vicky smiled.

Minutes later, the camp was buzzing with activity. Katie, who'd been perfecting her juggling at home, was keen to share her skills with the others. Unsurprisingly, Grace turned out to be brilliant at pulling scarves magically from her sleeves and then dancing around elegantly with them.

Ellie had discovered that diabolos were rubbery things a bit like two cups stuck together by their bottoms. You had to balance the diabolo on its middle on a special sort of rope and then spin it up in the air, before catching it back on the rope. It was hard, but she was beginning to get the hang of it.

Charlie was having a great time learning how to stilt walk on brightly-coloured upside-down flowerpots. She took it slowly at first, but was

soon going faster, and even tried hopping on one flowerpot foot!

Meantime, Jamila had decided to apply her musical skills to hoopla. She quickly worked out that if you got into a rhythm, you could keep the hoop spinning around your waist for quite a long time without dropping it. She wasn't sure she was ever going to be as good as Chloe and Sukia, though. They were able to spin hoops on their arms and legs as well!

The Brownies chatted and laughed as they practised. They were concentrating so hard on what they were doing that at first they didn't notice the large drops of rain that were splashing down on them.

"Quick!" said Sam. "Into the tents!"

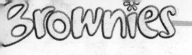

Fifteen minutes later, the rain was falling even harder. The Brownies used the time to write up their camp diaries, but once that was done, they got bored – and hungry too!

"It's a good job we've already made our picnic!" said Aruna, as she and Daisy raced from tent to tent to distribute lunch.

When they'd munched their way through the yummy sandwiches, the Brownies wondered what would happen next because it was still raining!

"Come on," the Camp Leaders said to each Six. "Get your coats on – we're off to the hall!"

"What about our circus stuff?" Molly asked.

"Don't worry," said Vicky. "We'll bring it all with us and carry on in the dry!"

Chapter 8

The Brownies shook off the rain and raced inside Waddow Hall.

"Phew!" said Jamila, as she sat down in the big room that Alex had led them to.

"I thought I was going to get soaked through all over again!" Ellie said.

Grace shivered. "I know what you mean."

"Wasn't it lucky we'd booked this room for the afternoon anyway," said Sam. "We must have known that it was going to rain!"

"Are we going to practise our circus skills some more?" asked Lauren.

"Yes," said Katie to the Leaders. "I saw that you'd brought the circus kit with you."

"In a little while," replied Vicky. "But we thought you'd like to make your collages and models first. That's why we booked this room – so you can work at the tables."

"Yay!" Ellie cheered.

So the Brownies arranged tables and chairs just like they did in the hall back in Badenbridge, and then Daisy handed out paper, glue and colouring pens. The girls were soon creating works of art.

Ellie had decided to make a tree out of her twigs. She tied them together with string so that the tree stood up on its own, and then hung a fantastic array of leaves from its branches. She worked happily, pleased that she'd decided to stay at camp.

The other Brownies created some terrific collages and models.

"Great work, girls," said Sam when they had finished.

"Yes," said Vicky. "We'd better put them away safely because we're going to return to our circus skills now!"

"But first, I've got some news about what we are going to do this evening," Sam said.

There was a murmur of excitement around the room.

"We thought you should perform a circus show for us this evening before supper," Vicky said, smiling.

"Yesss!" the Brownies cheered.

"We can pretend that our camp is really a Big Top!" explained Alex. "As long as it stops raining, of course…"

"We thought you would enjoy decorating

our camp to look like a circus, with posters and bright decorations," Sam added.

The excited Brownies agreed.

"We can spend the rest of the afternoon coming up with the acts," Vicky suggested. "Daisy has even brought some circus music to play in the background."

"And because you are all such stars, we thought your performance would be wasted if you only had a small audience," said Sam. "So we've invited our fellow campers across the field to come and enjoy the show too!"

"The Agnestown Brownies?" asked Katie. "Oh, they're really nice!"

"Don't circuses have a Ringmaster, Vicky?" Aruna wondered.

"They certainly do," Vicky replied. "Which is why I've brought a top hat and coat with me for our Ringmaster to wear!"

"Who's that going to be?" Jamila wanted to know.

"Boo would be brilliant!" said Molly. "Remember how good she was at our last Brownie show? She was really funny!"

"Hands up who thinks Boo should be our Ringmaster?" asked Sam.

Every Brownie in the room put up her hand.

"Looks like it's Boo, then!" announced Vicky. "Let's give her a clap!"

Boo blushed as everyone clapped.

Ellie grinned at her friends. She was having such a good time that she'd forgotten all about the muddy accident that had happened earlier.

"Let's hope it stops raining soon!" said Jamila. "We can't have a circus at the camp if it's still bucketing down…"

As the rain continued to pour down outside, the Brownies practised their circus skills in the dry and warmth of the hall.

The Foxes were going to juggle, whilst the Squirrels were stilt walking. The Rabbits had decided on a kind of conjuring show and the Hedgehogs were going to put on a diabolo display. Finally, the Badgers were practising a hoopla routine to music.

In the Foxes, Katie was so confident at juggling that she even attempted to do hoopla at the same time. She wobbled so much she got the giggles and ended up dropping her beanbags as well as the hoop.

Meanwhile, Boo was on one side of the room practising what she was going to say as she introduced the different Brownie acts.

The Camp Leaders decided to get in on the act as clowns. They pretended to throw buckets of water over Boo, and she stopped her speech to chase them around the room.

It was so funny that in the end, the other Brownies gradually stopped what they were doing to watch. They were in fits of laughter and, when Vicky, Sam, Alex, Aruna and

Daisy bowed to their audience, everyone clapped and cheered.

"Hey, it's stopped raining," Aruna said.

"Hooray!" everyone cheered.

"Does that mean we can go back to camp?" Ellie asked. "We need to start decorating it to look like a circus!"

"Good point," agreed Vicky. "We'd better take everything back with us."

"Come on then, girls!" said Sam. "Let's go!"

The Brownies decided to put their things back in the tents before they got on with making circus posters and banners. At the Hedgehogs' tent, Ellie was first inside.

"Oh no!" she exclaimed, as she sat on her camp bed. "Look at my sleeping bag! It's completely soaked…"

Chapter 9

"What's happened, Molly?" Ellie asked, as the Hedgehogs gathered around. None of the other sleeping bags in the tent were wet.

"Oh, I see what's gone wrong..." said Alex, who had followed the girls into their tent. "You've left it touching one of the tent walls. So the rain has poured down the side, and soaked into your sleeping bag and pyjamas."

Tears welled up in Ellie's eyes.

"Where am I going to sleep now?" she sobbed. "Oh, I'm no good at camping!"

The Hedgehogs sat outside their tent comforting Ellie, and Alex assured her that

they would be able to find her a dry sleeping bag. But Ellie was certain that she should just go home.

"OK," said Alex. "But I'm still going to see if I can sort out some new sleeping kit, just in case you change your mind."

Ellie's best friends came over to see her when they heard what had happened.

"Oh, Ellie!" said Jamila. "You can have my sleeping bag!"

"And my pyjamas," offered Grace.

"But where will you sleep then, Jamila?" puzzled Katie. "And what will you sleep in, Grace?" She pulled such a face that the other girls couldn't help but laugh. Even Ellie managed a smile.

"I'm going to call Mum," Ellie told them. "She'll come and get me."

"But we're only here for one more night," said Katie.

"Yes," said Grace. "And we need you for our Circus."

"We can't decorate camp without you!" Jamila added.

Ellie looked at them sadly, and sighed.

Before she could say anything, a lady arrived at camp with a sleeping bag under her arm.

She was wearing a name badge that said 'Gina'.

"One dry sleeping bag and extra Brownie sleepwear!" she said. "Which tent is it for?"

"This one, please," said Alex gratefully. "Thanks."

"Look," exclaimed Jamila. "Problem sorted!"

"Come on, Ellie. We need your help!" said Katie.

"Daisy's got all the paints and paper ready," Charlie said.

Slowly, Ellie smiled. "OK then." She looked round the camp. "I think we should start by making posters to put by the entrance to our site."

"Yesss!" cheered her friends. Ellie was staying!

The Brownies got busy painting. They created some wonderfully colourful posters and banners.

"Wow – the camp looks brilliant!" Izzy declared, as the Brownies stood back and admired their hard work. They'd put posters up all around the camp.

"Doesn't it?" said Grace.

"Hey!" exclaimed Katie. "Vicky and Sam are coming out of the Badgers' tent."

"It's another camp inspection." Aruna smiled. "I wonder who's won Beryl the Brownie this time?"

Katie wanted to rush into the Foxes' tent and check that it was OK but, before she could, Vicky and Sam came over and held up their right hands. The girls fell silent.

"Now, Brownies, we've just done another inspection to see how tidy you are keeping your tents."

She held up Beryl so that everyone could see her.

"The current holders of Beryl are the Foxes," she went on, "but the neatest tent today is…"

The Brownies waited nervously.

"…The Badgers'! Well done!"

The Brownies clapped as Izzy, the Badgers' Sixer, went up to receive Beryl.

"OK," said Vicky, looking at her watch. "Our audience will be here soon! So there's just enough time to paint clown faces on each other. Aruna and I have got some face paints – let's get started."

Vicky, Daisy and Aruna gave the Brownies some ideas about what colours to use, and soon there weren't any Brownies left in camp – they were all clowns!

Well, all but one. The only Brownie who hadn't become a clown was Boo, who had now dressed up in a tailcoat and her top hat. She looked terrific as the Ringmaster.

Boo had written a list of the different tricks and skills the Brownies were going to perform.

"OK," she said. "Does everyone know the order of our acts?"

The girls all nodded.

"I'll call you out into the ring when it's your turn!" Boo grinned excitedly.

"Hey, look!" said Jamila, pointing. "The Agnestown Brownies are arriving! Quick!"

The Agnestown Brownies were just as excited as the ones from Badenbridge.

They cheered as Boo appeared in the ring and announced the first act, which was Katie and the rest of the Foxes performing a juggling act. They'd got so good at it that

they even began to toss beanbags to each other as they juggled. And when any of them dropped one, they just clowned around as if it was meant to happen and made everyone laugh.

The Squirrels followed on with a stilt walking routine to music. Aruna started the music on the MP3 player, and the Squirrels were off! It was a good job that they all had clown smiles painted on their faces because Charlie and the others were concentrating so hard, they forgot to smile for real.

Then Boo came into the ring chased by the Camp Leaders, looking as if she was really in trouble. But then she made everyone laugh by chasing them out of the ring again! Boo asked the audience if they were enjoying the show and they cheered loudly.

Next, the Rabbits performed their magic act, producing scarves and juggling balls as if from nowhere. Grace even managed to trick some of the Brownies in the audience when she pretended to take scarves out of their Brownie clothes.

When the clapping had died down, Boo introduced the Hedgehogs, who performed an amazing display of diabolos and devil sticks, tossing and twirling them high above their heads. At one point, Ellie dropped her devil stick, but she put on a sad clown face and everyone cheered her on.

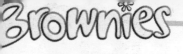

Boo chased the Hedgehogs out of the ring at the end of their act, and then told some jokes before asking the audience to welcome the last act – the Badgers.

The audience were sad that the show was coming to an end, but they soon cheered up when Jamila and the other Badgers raced into the ring to perform a dazzling display of hoopla. Izzy and Chloe had perfected the art

of spinning hoops around their arms at the same time as whizzing one around their waists. But the others weren't nearly as good, and instead got the audience laughing with them as they clowned around pretending to be truly bad at hoopla.

When Boo announced that the show had come to an end, there were cries of "No!" from the audience before they all rose to applaud. Jamila, Ellie, Charlie, Grace and Katie nudged each other and grinned.

"Well done, Brownies!" said Vicky and Sam, coming over to congratulate them.

"Wasn't it brilliant?" said Katie.

"Totally," Ellie replied.

"I loved it!" added Grace.

"I got some brilliant photos on your camera, Charlie," Daisy said, handing it over.

"Thanks so much!" Charlie grinned.

"So what are we doing now?" Katie asked the Leaders.

"I'm starving!" Jamila said.

"Me too!" agreed all the other Brownies.

Vicky and Sam laughed.

"We need everyone to help make our camp supper," Vicky said. "And the good news is that the Agnestown Brownies are going to join us!"

Chapter 10

With everyone helping, their campfire supper was soon cooked. They all tucked into a scrummy hotpot, followed by toasted marshmallows.

It was great to have a chance to get to know the Agnestown Brownies better, and everyone chatted and giggled. After supper, the Leaders led them all in singing, which was brilliant fun – especially when they split the camp into two groups and sang a round.

Before they knew it, it was time for bed.

"But we don't want to go to sleep!" said Ellie – who then yawned.

"Come on, you lot!" said one of the

115

Leaders of the Agnestown Brownies. "We need to get to bed. But before we go, let's take a group photo with our new friends!"

"Awww!" the Agnestown girls sighed, as they got ready to leave after the photo. They hugged their new friends goodbye, before slowly making their way across the field to their tents.

"That was the best night ever!" Molly said.

"Who's ready to go to the wash block?" asked Alex.

"Oh, do we have to wash?" Lucy wailed. "I'm too tired!"

"We can't go to bed looking like clowns!" Grace giggled. Lucy had completely forgotten she still had face paint on!

Alex laughed. "Come on – let's get sorted!"

The Brownies woke up late the next day.

"I can't believe it's already Sunday," sighed Jamila, as she tucked in to a bowl of porridge.

"Nor me!" agreed Katie.

"I know I kept saying before that I wanted to go home," Ellie said. "But now I'm having so much fun, I don't want to leave!"

The others laughed, but they knew exactly what she meant. Their first Brownie camp had been the best fun ever!

Once breakfast was cleared away and the washing-up done, the Brownies tidied the camp and packed their bags, ready for the journey home. Vicky and Sam did a final inspection, and this time Beryl the Brownie was awarded to the Hedgehogs. Then, all the Leaders went around the Sixes, checking the girls had completed their diaries and all their other badge work.

"Now," Vicky said, after calling the Brownies back to the Ring. "Let's have our final Pow Wow of camp."

"Aaaww!" the Brownies replied.

Vicky grinned. "I know it's sad, but we've had a good time, haven't we?"

"You've all worked hard and learned so many new things," Sam added. "Which is why we've got lots of badges to award!"

"Yesss!" the Brownies exclaimed.

"If you could line up behind your Sixers," Sam continued, "Alex will present you with your badges! Some of you will be getting your Out and about badges, others the Camper badge, and some the Camper advanced badge. Oh – and you are all getting your Circus performer badges too! Well done!"

After saying a last goodbye to the Agnestown Brownies, the 1st Badenbridge Brownies piled on to the bus to return home. As they drove away, they watched Waddow Hall disappear into the distance.

"Hands up who thought that was the best camp holiday ever?" asked Megan, the Sixer of the Squirrels.

"Me!" said every Brownie on the bus.

"Three cheers for Vicky, Sam, Alex, Aruna and Daisy!" declared Izzy, Sixer of the Badgers. "Hip Hip—"

"Hooray!" the Brownies cheered loudly.

The 1st Badenbridge Brownies were on their way home.

On Monday afternoon, Ellie, Jamila, Grace, Katie and Charlie met up in the adventure playground in the park. Still tired from their weekend, they were glad that it was half term and they didn't have to be in school. They sat on the tyre swings, chatting excitedly.

"I'm so glad you decided to stay at camp, Ellie," said Grace.

"Me too!" agreed Ellie. "And my mum said she was proud of me for not giving up after I got so wet and mucky!"

"That reminds me – I've brought my photos from camp," said Charlie. "Look!"

The five best friends giggled as they flipped through the pictures.

"I wish it was Brownies tomorrow night," sighed Ellie.

"But it's half term so we've got to wait a whole week," said Charlie.

"And there will be all the new girls joining at the next meeting too!" exclaimed Jamila.

"So there will be even more Brownies to have fun with!" said Katie. "I can't wait!"

"Nor me!" said Ellie. "But first, we've got an adventure playground to explore. Let's go!"

Meet all the 1st Badenbridge Brownies!

Pip

Lottie

Katie

Amber

Emma

Caitlin

Lucy

Grace

Molly

Boo

Poppy

Amy

Ellie

Lauren

Sukia

Holly

Jasmine

Jamila

Izzy

Chloe

Ashvini

Faith

Charlie

Bethany

Megan

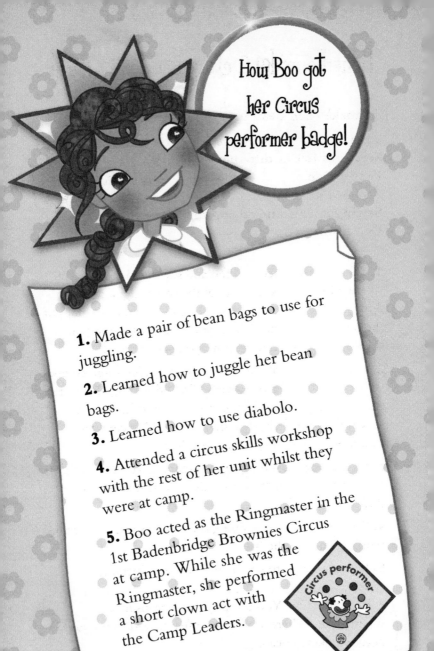

How Boo got her Circus performer badge!

1. Made a pair of bean bags to use for juggling.

2. Learned how to juggle her bean bags.

3. Learned how to use diabolo.

4. Attended a circus skills workshop with the rest of her unit whilst they were at camp.

5. Boo acted as the Ringmaster in the 1st Badenbridge Brownies Circus at camp. While she was the Ringmaster, she performed a short clown act with the Camp Leaders.

Circus performer

How to make a Juggling Bean Bag!

To make each bean bag you will need:

2 pieces of felt about 16cm x 10cm
Scraps of felt in different colours
Fabric glue
A pencil
Sewing needle and strong thread
Dried beans

1. Take the two pieces of felt and sew them together up the two long edges and one of the short edges. If you don't want to sew, you could stick the same three sides of the felt together with fabric glue – but make sure you wait for the glue to dry before you get to step 3!

2. Cut the scraps of felt into shapes and glue them to one or both sides of the bean bag. The Badenbridge Brownies cut their shapes into eyes, noses, and mouths to make clown faces for their bags, but you could make stars or moons – or any other shapes you like!

3. Fill the bag with the beans so that it is about two thirds full. Be careful not to overfill the bag or it will be difficult to juggle.

4. Sew or glue the remaining short edge so that the beans won't fall out of the bag.

5. Leave the glue to dry before you start juggling!

★ **Brownie Tip:** You can buy dried beans in any supermarket. There are lots of different sorts – try aduki beans or kidney beans.

Collect all the books in the series!

Got it! ◯

Got it! ◯

Got it! ◯

Got it! ◯

Got it! ◯

And look out for...

Brownies
christmas cheer

Christmas is coming, and the 1st Badenbridge Brownies are getting in the spirit of things! With crafts to make for the local Christmas market, festive goodies to bake for the unit party, and a trip to the local pantomime to look forward to, the girls eagerly set about spreading Christmas cheer. Now, if only it would snow…

Join the Brownies

Brownies do it all!

They do cool things to get badges like the Artist badge and the Computer badge, they have sleepovers, they make heaps of friends and have lots of fun.

Brownies are aged from seven to ten and are part of Girlguiding UK, the largest organization for girls and young women in the UK, which has around 575,000 members.

To learn more about what Brownies get up to, visit www.girlguiding.org.uk/brownies or call 0800 169 5901 to find out how you can join in the fun.